A Verse

to

Christmas

Rocky Mountain Christmas Train
Book Two

Roxy Boroughs

A Verse
to
Christmas

Roxy Boroughs

—A Verse to Christmas—

—Rocky Mountain Christmas Train, Book Two—

Published November 2024

by Baucis & Philemon and Donna Tunney

ISBN: 978-1-7777555-4-6 Digital Edition 1

ISBN: 978-1-7777555-5-3 Digital Edition 2

ISBN: 978-1-7777555-6-0 (Print Edition)

Cover art by Kelly Moran

Copyediting by Terri St. Clair & Ted Williams

Dedication

To B.
And my train besties—Raine, Ellen, Shawna,
and my partner in all things train, Katie.

A Verse to Christmas

Davyn Kayne was the shining star of the literary world, until a rival's false accusation toppled his career.

Waitress Paige Chamberlain has lived a more mundane life but hides a secret that could ruin them both.

Can two mismatched strangers, averse to the holidays, discover the true meaning of Christmas and make poetry together?

The News Post

Charity Train Rolls This December.

Win the trip of a lifetime this December on the maiden voyage of the luxurious Rocky Mountain Christmas Train. With a chance to win a $25,000 cash prize for the charity of your choice. To enter, send your name, address, and a bio, along with the name of your charity and why you chose it to 3566 Maple Lane, Delta, Alabama, 36258.

Rocky Mountain Christmas Train

Chapter One

After three days of traveling on the super fancy Rocky Mountain Christmas Train, Paige Chamberlain was eager to get out and stretch her legs.

Most days, she was on her feet, serving customers at the Over Easy Diner where she worked in her hometown of Wamsutter, Wyoming. The place had a skatepark, a trailer court, and not much else. It sat beside Interstate 80, a major highway from San Francisco, through Cheyenne, to the East Coast.

Paige had visited Cheyenne a time or two, but never California. She'd never even been out of Wyoming!

Until now.

In her twenty-six years, this was her first time leaving the state, on her trip of a lifetime, which began in Denver, Colorado. Ironically, the train was clickety-clacking back through Wyoming on this epic journey she'd won.

And she'd never won anything before in her life! All thanks to an unknown benefactor.

Finally, she'd see the rest of her state and more as they continued north. Somewhere along the way, she and another contestant would work together to complete a task of some sort for a chance to win the twenty-five thousand dollar grand prize.

Tonight, everyone had been invited to enjoy an off-train excursion, in the shadow of Casper Mountain. With the soft snow falling around them, in a state where the wind could pick up at any moment, they were shuttled to an auditorium.

As Paige passed through the entrance, she caught her reflection in the glass doors—a dark-haired, wide-eyed gal, in well-worn jeans and an oversize parka. She burrowed into the coat's warmth as the crowd swept her inside.

Once in the bright airy foyer, she eyed the ginormous Christmas tree in the corner to her right. Dressed in blue lights, red baubles, and white tinsel, it brightly displayed the colors of both the country and the state's flags. The latter flapped from the diner's flagpole every day. But the image of a white bison in silhouette, surrounded by blue, and trimmed with red and white borders, wasn't anywhere near as fancy as this Christmas tree.

Stunning.

Paige never bothered putting up a tree in her apartment. Decorating the diner was more than enough work. But she admired those who made an extra effort and strung outdoor lights on their houses and displayed blow-up Santas on their lawns. It all added to the festive mood of the neighborhood.

She stood on tiptoes, scanned the folks wearing suits and evening gowns, and looked for a familiar face.

Chris Watson, an elderly gentleman, rolled his wheelchair up to the Christmas tree, with his personal nurse, Maddie Hayes, by his side. A middle-aged couple, who always dressed identically, joined them. Tonight, the pair wore matching green sweaters. His read, "I have everything I want for Christmas," and hers read, "I'm everything."

Awwwww.

By a bank of eight-foot windows, Jenny, their hostess, chatted with two men and four women that Paige also recognized from the train.

Would one of them be her partner?

"Looking for the loo?" an accented voice at her side asked. Bruce, a bartender from the train, used his blond head to point toward the washrooms. Despite his Aussie expressions, Paige could relate to Bruce as a fellow server. He'd come to her rescue one evening during a fancy train dinner when she didn't know which fork to use.

And, now that he'd mentioned it, a trip to the ladies' room before the presentation might be a good idea.

"Thanks. Are you staying for the show?" She'd feel more comfortable sitting with someone she knew. In his usual train uniform of a white shirt, black pants, and a black tie, he was better dressed for the event than she was.

"Can't. Just here to shepherd people in, then it's back to the Christmas Train for me. You can join the staff in the bar car after the show if you like."

Page wasn't much of a drinker. She'd nurse the same glass all night, just to be sociable. "I'll keep that in mind."

Bruce smiled, his eyes crinkling. As he strode off, an usher handed her a program, which promised *An Evening of Christmas Poetry and*

Song. Paige liked music, but she'd never been one to read a poem, not even when she attended high school.

Which made it even more curious when she'd found a book of poems in her cabin on the train earlier this evening.

She pulled the copy from the purse she'd slung over her shoulder and randomly flipped to the copyright page. "Third edition."

She hadn't meant to say the words out loud and, when the woman beside her gave her a sharp look, Paige made a mental note. *Read with your eyes and not your mouth.*

She stepped away from the woman, found a quiet corner, and studied the book's cover again. Davyn Kayne's bearded face peered out at her.

An award-winning, bestselling poet, his biography said. *Today's top recording artists have set his poems and original lyrics to music, resulting in eight Number One Hits, two Grammys, a Golden Globe, and an Oscar. Davyn Kayne is simply a global phenomenon.*

Who could live up to such hype?

And who could have dropped the book off in her cabin? One of the housekeeping staff? Did they enjoy poetry? Would they miss it?

When she got back to the train, she'd ask for the Lost and Found. She hadn't had time on her way to the auditorium, so she'd stuffed the book in her purse.

Oh, who was she kidding?

She could have left the book in her cabin, but something about the photo intrigued her. The author reminded her of someone she'd seen before. And a story she'd heard. On the news, maybe.

A bell sounded and the foyer lights dimmed for a second. The audience moved toward two sets of gigantic double doors that led to the seating area. Wary of being engulfed by the crowd, Paige hung back.

That's when she noticed a man leaning against a pillar. Or trying to hide behind it.

As a waitress, she'd learned to size up people fast and predict her tip from a customer's clothes and attitude with uncanny accuracy. Single, middle-aged men were often generous. Young couples with kids? Forget about it.

This guy was in his mid-thirties. Dark, unruly hair fell across his forehead. The man's tan suede jacket spoke of money but was far too light for a Wyoming winter. The inner corners of his brows drew upward and made his dark eyes appear sunken. His mouth sloped down at the sides like he'd forgotten how to smile.

She'd seen him on the train and recognized him as a passenger. Another contestant, like herself, perhaps.

He took a step toward the auditorium, froze, then turned and headed for the doors she'd just entered, and fled the building, into the night.

Through the windows, she saw him pull a black scarf over his mouth. With that cloth covering the lower part of his face, the man looked very much like...

No. It wasn't possible. Too coincidental.

Paige looked at the photo on the book's cover again. Could the man really be Davyn Kayne?

Chapter Two

Back in his cabin on the train, Davyn awoke. He rubbed his neck, stiff from sleeping upright in his black leather chair.

With a groan, he leaned his elbows on the desk at his side and sent an empty bourbon glass skittering. The sweet vanilla scent of the liquor's residue turned his stomach, and the knock at his door reverberated in his head.

"Come."

The cabin door slid open and Bruce, the bartender, appeared. He looked crisp and perky—too perky, frankly—in a clean, white shirt. Had the dear lad come to bring him the *hair of the dog* that bit him? It might be the best remedy for Davyn's condition.

After singing out a cheery greeting, Bruce shot a glance at the bed, yesterday's Belgian chocolate still sitting on the crisp, white pillowcase. Without comment, he set a tray on the mahogany desk, next to the eight-inch miniature Christmas tree that decorated the room.

Davyn planned to chuck the fake pine in a drawer as soon as he was alone.

On the tray, he eyed a cup of black coffee, a large glass of water, a serving of multigrain toast and, beside the napkin...a couple of Tylenol.

Was it that obvious he needed them?

He glimpsed his reflection in the cabin's panoramic window—his jaw in need of a razor, his eyes rimmed red, and his clothes unchanged since yesterday.

Yup. It was that obvious.

"On the Rocky Mountain Christmas Train, we strive to meet your every need," Bruce told him. "Even before you think of it."

Though the spiel sounded a tad rehearsed, Davyn had to admit, he sure hadn't wanted for anything on this trip so far. Meals on the train were top-notch and the views of the passing snow-covered countryside, gorgeous. He stood, unsteady as a rooky sailor, and reached into his back pocket.

"No gratuity needed."

"Right." Just as well. He'd spent months in court hemorrhaging the money he'd earned from his first book. First and last. If Davyn hadn't won this trip, he'd never have been able to afford it.

A squeak sounded on the other side of the cabin wall. *No,* not a squeak. More of a yip.

"Is there a dog onboard?"

"Yeah. Fellow next door has a right cutie. The organizers told him to bring the dog along. Knew he shouldn't be without it."

The dog yapped again, and Bruce smiled. Indulgently. Or, Davyn wondered, was that tolerance directed at him?

Before he could ask, Bruce palmed the empty bourbon glass, backed out of the cabin saying, "Enjoy your breakfast," and closed the door behind him.

In Davyn's current state, eating was the last thing on his mind, but he knew he needed some carbs and *non-alcoholic* liquid. He took a steadying breath and removed the holly-themed ring from his napkin.

That's when he saw the cream envelope embossed with gold lettering. From it, he pulled out a note.

Dear Davyn:

Please join us in the forward observation car at 9:00 a.m. to meet your partner and hear about your challenge.

Warmest holiday regards and blessings of the season.

Your hostess,
Jenny

"The observation car, huh?" Davyn blinked to get his watch in focus.

He had an hour to down his breakfast and get himself together. Fortunately, the stateroom came with everything, including a minibar, a heated floor in the small but luxurious bathroom, and a complimentary Turkish cotton robe.

Maybe a shower would make him feel like a normal human being again. That or another shot of bourbon.

The dog next door gave another little yelp, as if in agreement.

Chapter Three

Paige slid into one of the few empty seats alongside her fellow contestants in the glass-domed observation car. In her hand, she still clutched the note that told her to come and meet her partner.

Outside the enormous windows, rural Wyoming whizzed past. Rugged, unsettled land lay cradled by the surrounding snow-topped mountains. Above her, the clear sky capped off everything with a deep shade of blue, only seen in winter.

From her cushy leather perch, Paige thanked her good fortune at scoring such a classy ride, as she admired the car's oak and mahogany interior. Not to mention the gleaming brass accents, polished to such a shine she could see her reflection. Today, she'd spruced up her clothes to better fit her accommodations and wore her best dress pants and a red sweater with dainty white snowflakes across the yoke.

The car was decorated with snowflakes too—crocheted, sugar-starched ones that, along with glass ornaments, hung from evergreen boughs and strings of tiny lights—all carefully arranged so as not to obstruct the views.

At the front of the car, Jenny, in her customary Mrs. Claus costume, leafed through several pages of notes. Seemingly satisfied with their order, she tapped them on the portable wooden podium. "Good morning, everyone."

The crowd's murmurs grew softer. Several folks shushed the ones still talking. Once everyone was quiet, Jenny resumed speaking.

"Thank you for your attention. As you probably know by now, I'm Jenny, your hostess."

A round of applause interrupted her. She blushed, took off her gold-rimmed glasses, and polished the lenses on the shoulder of her blouse—though Paige suspected the young woman didn't need the glasses to see. They were just part of her costume.

"Like our first group of contenders, you'll be assigned a partner, a team name, and a task to complete within a particular timeframe—all prepared by our mystery benefactor. The clock will start ticking right after breakfast."

So far on the trip, the team names had suited the competitors. One of the first was called Triple Threat, because there were three in the team—Seth Mathison, a fireman, Joy Spencer, an office manager, and her daughter, Chantal. Paige had first noticed the cute, spunky seven-year-old because she used arm support poles due to her cerebral palsy. Together, the three had taken over the staging of a Christmas concert and play.

Paige couldn't imagine doing something like that. As a kid, she'd performed in only one play, which was one too many for her.

"If you're successful," Jenny went on, "you'll be able to sit back and enjoy the rest of the trip without a care in the world. And anticipate our final draw for the grand prize winners to donate to the charity of their choice. If you exhibit poor sportsmanship, or for any other reason are disqualified," she said, her tone pointed, "you'll be asked to leave the train."

The exact fate of Team Rancy from the last group of contestants. Their task of finding a hundred people to donate money to a local library ended when another passenger discovered them cheating. Paige hadn't heard how the teammates, Randy and Nancy, had tried to fix the outcome. Maybe they were short on their goal and threw their own money in the donation bucket. They'd probably thought that investing a handful of their own bucks would be worth it for a chance to win the grand prize.

"Now," Jenny continued, drawing Paige back to the present. "Please stand when I call your names."

The first couple, both fit women in their fifties named Mia, were dubbed Team Mama Mias. Jenny's mention of their former friendship and subsequent split led the two to lob snide comments at one another about their children's sports rivalry during grade school.

Jenny held up her hands like a referee. "Thank you, ladies. Time to end this... er... discussion... and announce your challenge." She consulted her notes. "Mias, you will create an original Christmas game. One suitable for kids of all ages."

The first Mia grunted, and the second rolled her eyes. "Onto the next team," Jenny announced, moving right along.

She singled out a man and a woman and dubbed them the Team Stirs. Chuckles followed the pun, a welcome relief after the tension of the last few minutes.

"Team Stirs, you're tasked with beating the Guinness World Record for making the largest sticky toffee pudding. The biggest currently on record," Jenny informed them, "weighed over seven hundred pounds."

The crowd oohed and aahed.

If this food theme kept up, Paige would have no problem. She often worked the grill when Rosie, the sixty-some-year-old owner and chief cook at the Over Easy, left early or went on holidays.

"Our final contestants are..." Jenny flipped through her paperwork. "Paige Chamberlain and Davyn Kayne."

"Huh?" The air whooshed from Paige's lungs.

Davyn Kayne?! Had she misheard the name? Was he really on the train? Had she truly spotted him the night before?

Jenny peered over her glasses at her audience. "Could the two of you please stand?"

Paige rose, taking her time to look for Davyn on the way up. He stood at the back of the car, leaning against a seat, his face pale. Hopefully, he could hold a spatula as well as he held a pen.

"From now on, we'll call the two of you, Team Rhyme and Dine. You're tasked with writing an original, family-friendly Christmas poem, along the lines of *A Visit from St. Nicholas*.

"And you'll need to complete it by noon tomorrow."

Rocky Mountain
Christmas Train

Chapter Four

P aige fought a rush of tears—right there, in the observation car, in front of everyone. Those waterworks followed her to the dining car as she waited for Davyn Kayne to arrive at her table to discuss strategies.

How could she admit to him—*to everyone!*—that she was doomed to fail? That she'd cause him a disqualification.

She grabbed a fistful of the dangling tablecloth and held on tight. She might need to use it as a hanky. But she'd have to be careful not to tug on it too hard. She might tip over the glass bowl centerpiece filled with mini red and gold Christmas balls.

"May I?"

Paige looked up, way up, at the tall man who'd appeared beside her.

His hair was still messy, though damp, as if he'd recently showered. Maybe he was just one of those guys whose hair had a mind of its own.

It suited him. Gave him a rebellious look.

That edginess continued with his clothes—all black—from his jeans to the light cashmere turtleneck that hugged his torso. Page licked her lips and forced her gaze higher.

She'd first thought his eyes were brown but, now that she saw him up close, they looked more hazel. The sort of eyes that could be brown one minute and greenish the next. He held Jenny's invitation but flipped it onto the table as he took the seat across from Paige.

"I'm Davyn, by the way." With his deep voice, the man could have been a radio announcer on an easy-listening station.

"I know."

His eyes narrowed, then he nodded. "Of course. Jenny called our names."

He said it as if he didn't realize he was famous. Or infamous. To prove the point, she pulled his book from her purse and set it on the table.

After the presentation in the auditorium last night, she'd read his work. Or as much of it as she could understand. Then she'd searched for information about him on her phone. "You're a poet."

"Was."

"You don't write anymore?" Maybe she wasn't the only one about to let the team down. "I thought that was something people were born to do."

"I used to think so too."

Before the court case. He didn't say it, but Paige could read between the lines. His book had been wildly successful. There was even talk of a movie deal and a Broadway musical. Until the accusations two Christmases ago.

Of *plagiarism*.

She'd never seen the word before. Had to get her phone to pronounce it for her. Then she'd looked up the definition. *To commit literary theft. To pass off the words of another as your own.*

"How about you? What's your name again?"

She let go of the tablecloth and rubbed her hand on her pant leg. "Paige."

He chuckled.

"Is my name funny to you?"

"Under the circumstances." He sipped his water and grimaced. "Do you have a last name, Paige?"

"Doesn't everyone?"

"Unless you're a rock star like Cher or Rihanna."

He'd probably met them too, along with Adele and Madonna. The man did own two Grammys, after all. "I'm not much of a singer."

"Me, neither." His brows lifted, quizzically. "So, what's your last name?"

"It's Chamberlain."

"Ah. The Lord Chamberlain's Men—Shakespeare's company. Good ol' Will wrote some of his greatest plays for them, including *Hamlet*."

What was he on about? Couldn't he talk like a normal person? Instead of Rhyme and Dine, maybe Jenny should have called them Egghead and Jughead.

"And, since I've surmised you're not a rock star, what is it you do, Paige Chamberlain?"

"I'm a waitress." Talk about normal.

"Of course. You're the *Dine* portion of Team Rhyme and Dine. *Server* would be the politically correct term."

Oh, dear. Was he one of those woke people? "How about hash-slinger?"

"Nice play on words," he noted, "given our current location in gunslinging, cowboy country."

True, the Cowboy State was Wyoming's nickname. Also true, the wordplay was accidental, but she had no plans to confess that.

"So, my hash-slinging buckaroo," he crooned. "Were you born to it?"

Born to waitress? To clean up other people's messes? To scrape hardened gum off the underside of tables? To have fifty-year-old men pat her bottom? To deal with customers demanding refunds because the beef burger they'd ordered and devoured wasn't vegan?

Not likely!

As if anyone aspired to waitressing. It was usually Plan B or C. Or something to do to earn money while you were waiting for a better plan to pan out.

But Paige had never had a better plan.

She swung her legs out from under the table and stood. "Excuse me, but I'm not anyone's buckaroo." If she'd been serving this smart-mouthed Davyn-guy, she would have been tempted to spit in his food.

She took two quick steps away. When he caught her arm, she turned, ready to put him in his place.

"I thought, perhaps, your parents owned a restaurant," he said.

She pursed her lips. Was that really what he meant?

"Most people in the U.S. earn their living in the service industry," he reported, as if delivering the news. "The country would fall apart without them. Without you. I meant no offense."

Had she taken it when none was intended?

She reran their conversation in her mind. Had she overreacted? Imagined that he'd insulted her profession because she thought so little of it herself?

Maybe.

Since now, any superiority he'd displayed was gone. He looked up at her, his eyes filled with regret. And something else.

Defeat.

"I know I don't deserve it, but I'd like you to give me another chance."

Was he sincere? Or was he being nice now because he wanted an opportunity to win the grand prize?

While she weighed the options, Paige glanced at Bruce, who'd appeared with a tray filled with glasses of ice water. He gave her a tight smile and began doling out drinks to the patrons seated at the opposite table.

Did the Aussie know something about Davyn that she didn't? And why was Bruce serving during breakfast, anyway? That wasn't the bartender's usual job. Cliff O'Reilly, the red-headed Irishman, was her regular breakfast server.

When Davyn gave a soft tug on Paige's arm, her attention turned back to him. Should she give him another chance? Trust the remorse she saw in those hazel eyes?

She'd shown him the line. It wasn't likely he'd try to cross it again. If he did, Paige would ask for a different partner.

She might anyway. Or he might. Once he knew her secret.

Chapter Five

Davyn realized he was still holding her arm. He let go and Paige slipped from his grasp. She clutched the place where his hand had rested a moment ago and stepped back. She'd either leave or stay now, but he hoped she'd stay.

She had a down-to-earth prettiness he hadn't seen in a long while. Not when celebrities glommed onto him, shot so full of Botox and fillers they looked like alien creatures.

Not so Paige Chamberlain. She possessed an expressive make-up-free face, big green eyes, and wore her brown hair in a practical high ponytail.

Very pretty.

She resumed her seat, and he let out the breath he'd been holding. "Thanks." As Bruce rushed by, Davyn caught his attention. "A coffee, please. Black."

Bruce's eyes opened wide, the whites showing, and then he jogged off. What had the young man so panicked about coffee?

When Davyn focused on Paige again, he found her staring at his book. With all the picturesque scenery passing by, she was gazing at the dreaded tome. If the window beside him had opened, he'd have thrown the bloody book out in the snow.

"You were accused of—"

"*Accused*, yes. Lots of people are accused of things they didn't do."

She pursed her lips as she mulled over his words. Then she picked up the book and examined both sides. "How long does it take to write something like this?"

He could use his standard Hemingwayesque answer, claiming he'd 'banged away at the keyboard for years with an open vein,' but he doubted she'd believe such romanticized nonsense. She'd already called him out once.

And she'd been right about that waitressing crack he'd made, being born to it and all. He'd meant the comment as a joke. At her expense. A *quid pro quo*. A sour jab to match his sour mood.

He'd assumed she'd give back as good as she got. Then he'd seen the insecurity in her eyes, the self-doubt. He wasn't ready to risk another smart-aleck remark. Not with her.

He shifted the festive centerpiece closer to the window, so one less thing separated them.

"It took all my life, really. Everything I'd lived up to then went into the book. But the actual writing of words came quickly. Within a few weeks."

Her large eyes grew wider. "Really?"

"I think that creates the best kind of writing. When it flows out of you. Songwriters will say the same. A few minutes is all it takes to write some of the greatest hits." He smoothed a wrinkle from the tablecloth. "Of course, revisions follow."

"I can't imagine."

"It's not everyone's cup of tea. Or coffee," he quipped, as Bruce arrived with his steaming cup of Joe—almost as much liquid in the saucer as in the cup.

The smoky scent of bacon from the kitchen car wafted by, and Davyn's stomach growled. He scanned the tables, but none of the other passengers had received their meals either, though it was well past ten o'clock. Heck, Davyn hadn't even seen today's breakfast menu.

Pinch-faced patrons fixed hard gazes at Bruce. What the heck was the delay?

With that voice of his, Paige could have listened to Davyn all day. But she had to confess her secret to him. Before this went any further.

Throat dry, she took a sip of water and swirled it around her mouth before swallowing.

"Look...I'm going to level with you. I don't know the first thing about writing a poem."

The guy didn't bat an eye. "Probably a good thing. You'll give the project a new perspective, a fresh approach. As the Zen master said, 'In the beginner's mind, there are many possibilities, but in the expert's, there are few.'"

Zen master? Seriously? How could they write a poem together if they didn't even speak the same language? She braced both palms on the table. "No. I mean, I really can't do this challenge. I'll talk to Jenny. Get you a different partner."

"I don't want a different partner."

Was the man thick? Or just obstinate? Still, deep down, a part of her felt touched by his loyalty. "That's very sweet of you to say, but honestly, I'd be dead weight. You write the poem."

"Not me. I haven't written a word in two years. You write it."

"Me?" she squeaked. "I flunked Grade 10 English." And promptly dropped out of high school. "I c-can't write a poem in twenty-four hours. I c-couldn't write one if they gave m-me twenty-four *years.*" There, her secret was out. And darn it, her stutter was back too. She took a deep breath to calm herself.

"If I may," said Bruce, appearing at their table. "You're a team. You must work on your task together. That's the point."

Great. It was on the tip of her tongue to say, 'Thanks for nothing, buddy,' when she noticed the perspiration on his forehead. "What's the problem, Bruce?"

He sighed. "The regular server is down with a migraine."

"What about the other bartender?" A hearty gal, as far as Paige knew. "Can't she help?"

"Twyla? She's serving in one of the other dining cars. We're short-staffed there too."

"And you're trying to do everything here on your own?" There had to be at least thirty patrons in this dining car. Probably more.

Bruce shrugged. "There's no one else."

Paige took another bracing gulp of water and stood. "Oh, yes, there is."

Davyn's jaw went slack as his new partner shot out of her seat and, after a quick huddle with Bruce, began helping with the breakfast rush. She took orders, ran them to the kitchen car, and headed back with steaming plates of bacon and eggs, smoked salmon, fruit, pastries, and morning mimosas.

Davyn resisted the urge to order one.

He'd waited tables back in his college days. For a week. He'd messed up orders, dropped plates, and spilled coffee on customers. He quit before they could fire him.

Paige Chamberlain put him to shame. The motion of the train didn't jar her. She remained cool under pressure, executing her movements with controlled precision and grace. If Tchaikovsky's *The Nutcracker* had a restaurant scene, and Paige was a server, she'd be the prima ballerina.

Perhaps she was born to it, after all.

Chapter Six

Davyn crumpled another napkin filled with inky chicken scratches.

He sat in the bar car with Paige, the small round table between them littered with pens, paper napkins, and cardboard coasters embossed with the train's image.

All contained scattered words and phrases. All garbage.

The click-clack of the train as it rushed through Wyoming provided a steady beat, a rhythm that should have made their poetry-writing task easier. But it was proving as difficult as scaling one of those mountains they passed.

Maybe the pianist was distracting him. One-third of the train's jazz trio, Jamila Scott, a gorgeous black musician from Chicago, played Christmas songs, pianissimo.

Maybe the car itself claimed his attention, with its salmon-colored seats and oak paneling. Rows of stained-glass transoms hung above the enormous picture windows—all trimmed with garlands of gold tinsel. *Exquisite.*

Or maybe it was the thought of all that liquor behind the bar.

He sat back in his seat and cracked his neck with a satisfying pop. What was he balking at? All they had to do was knock off a poem. *One* poem! How difficult could it be? Infinitely easier than putting on a show like one of the last teams. He and Paige were getting off light by comparison. No one would ever have to read the schlock they produced.

Together, they'd already composed:

Christmas comes but once a year,
Bringing with it lots of cheer.
Until the costs of presents soar,
And help reduce your credit score.

And:

Christmas brings us tasty treats,
Cookies, candies—tons of sweets,
I prefer a shot of rum,
In my rum-tum-tummy, tum-tum.

Granted, he'd added the last two lines both times, though Paige did all the writing. He hadn't picked up a pen since the accusations hit him the Christmas before last. Hadn't composed a poem—not even a grocery list.

Doubted he ever would again.

Still, he didn't want to see Paige fail their challenge because of him. He'd taught enough students that, if nothing else, he could mentor her while she wrote the poem.

But a poem to *Christmas?*

He knew Paige was trying her best but, besides his newfound aversion to writing, they both had very different, very superficial views of the holiday.

"We're approaching this the wrong way," he said, chucking their last attempt in the small garbage can Bruce had provided for them. "What does Christmas mean to you personally, Paige? How do you celebrate?"

"I don't." She straightened their stack of paper napkins. A stalling tactic, he recognized. "I'm always working right until the holiday. Then, on the twenty-fifth, all I want to do is relax on the couch in my PJs. I reheat turkey leftovers from the diner for supper."

"No big family dinner?"

"My mom died when I was a kid. My dad married again and started a new family. Five years ago, he moved to Colorado for work. I always send him a Christmas card but, last year, I got it back. He'd moved and forgot to tell me."

While speaking, she'd singled out one napkin and had absently ripped it into little pieces.

"That's rough."

"He's not a bad person, just not great at juggling." Noticing the mess she'd made, Paige collected the scraps of paper and threw them into the trash. "I heard from him after the New Year."

"It must hurt, though."

She shrugged. "How about you? Got family?"

He hesitated, debating how much to tell her. She'd opened up to him and shared a personal story. It was only fair he reciprocated.

"My parents kicked me out of the house when I was eighteen after I told them I planned to try my luck at poetry. They thought that meant I aspired to be a bum, and they wanted to teach me a lesson. When I was successful and the money started rolling in, they contacted me. Hinted that they needed a new car."

Her eyes widened. "Did you buy them one?"

"Two. One each."

"And?"

"When my career went south, so did they."

"Ghosted." She clasped his forearm—a sympathetic gesture.

When he looked down at her hand, he saw he was clutching his water glass, his knuckles white. He released it and focused on their connection. Her touch felt good, comforting. He could grow to like it. Expect it.

"Yeah. Too bad we aren't writing a Halloween poem."

He'd hoped to lighten the mood, but she didn't fall for his attempt at humor. She gave his arm a reassuring squeeze.

Somehow, the simple contact made up for all those holidays he'd spent alone. Often alone in a crowd, with people he barely knew clamoring around him, wanting to step into his orbit.

Until that orbit decayed.

This holiday, she was here with him, committed to their task, despite her insecurities. He wasn't about to fail her.

That's when the solution came to him. He smacked his free hand against the table. "No wonder we're having trouble. How can we write a verse to Christmas when we're *averse* to Christmas? We need to get in the festive mood. And we need an angle."

She inched forward. "An angle?"

"A point. We need to come up with a unique statement about Christmas that no one has said before."

Paige's shoulders slumped. "That's a tall order."

Yes. With all the songs, poems, and Hallmark movies out there, it *was* a tall order. Maybe an impossible one. How were they supposed to explore the holiday season on a train with intermittent access to Wi-Fi?

Bruce appeared at their table and refilled their supply of ice water and napkins. "We'll be making a stopover at Pinecone, Wyoming, in twenty minutes for those who want to disembark and do some shopping."

They thanked the bartender and sipped their waters in silence until Davyn leaped up. "Let's get our coats."

Paige stared at him, her mouth forming the sweetest O. "We don't have time to sightsee. We've got to write this poem."

He took her hand and pulled her up. "Our first step is research."

"Research?" Without letting go, she reached back and grabbed her purse. "What do we need to research?"

"Christmas."

Rocky Mountain
Christmas Train

Chapter Seven

True to its name, Pinecone, Wyoming, was a sweet, little, mountain town with snow-covered pine trees everywhere. The place was out of a storybook and reminded Paige of Stars Hollow from the TV show *Gilmore Girls*. It even had a small park in the center of town with a charming gazebo for its some 10,000 residents to enjoy.

Dressed up for Christmas, Pinecone's storefronts sported wreaths, garlands, sparkling lights, and Santas, while garlands of tinsel coiled around every lamppost. They shimmered red, gold, and green in the sunlight.

Out of the corner of her eye, Paige caught Davyn shivering. "That light jacket isn't right for this weather. The first thing we should do is get you a proper winter coat."

He huddled inside his outerwear. "Usually, this sees me through the worst of the season."

"In Los Angeles," Paige pointed out. "You're in Wyoming now." She scanned the downtown area and found exactly what they needed. "Look, the local thrift store."

Page pointed to a place called Seconds on First. It sat right on the corner of First and Main, just across the street from where they stood.

She took a step to cross the intersection and noticed Davyn wasn't by her side. She glanced back in time to notice his features tighten before he masked his expression.

Was he reacting to the cold? Or something else? Paige loved the thrill of hunting for thrift store bargains. Maybe Davyn had grown accustomed to the money that went with his celebrity status.

"No sense spending a lot on something you're going to wear for a couple of weeks. It's not like you need a parka in California."

He struck a smile, but Paige sensed it was forced.

They made their way across the street and inside the store where Davyn bought himself a gently used, khaki, down-filled parka for the price of the turkey dinner special at the Over Easy.

Dressed for the cold, they strolled around the town until they found a bookstore. Paige, knowing she was a liability for the team, browsed the literary section and found the perfect research item. A rhyming dictionary.

"I didn't even know there were such things," she confessed, as they exited the store. The dictionary also contained a section that defined poetic terms and included examples of iambic pentameter, haiku, and assonance—words she'd completely forgotten from her high school lessons, if she ever knew them at all. "I noticed a lot of the poems in your book didn't rhyme."

He gripped her elbow and helped her dodge a puddle. "It's not a prerequisite."

"But we were trying to come up with rhymes on the train."

"Our challenge is to write a family-oriented poem. I think most people will expect it to rhyme. That's why I picked up a copy of *A Visit from St. Nicolas* to inspire us." He fished it out of the bag the store clerk had given him.

Paige scooted to one side of the busy sidewalk so she could stop and look at the thin hardcover. A big, color picture of Santa in his sleigh, pulled by reindeer, graced the cover.

"Written by Clement Clarke Moore," she said, reading the author's name. She opened the book and saw the first line. "When Jenny mentioned this poem, I didn't realize she meant *'Twas the Night Before Christmas.'* The edition showed a photo of Moore's handwritten copy.

"I also picked up a couple of notebooks for us and a pad of foolscap," Davyn added. "Now, we can jot down our ideas without depleting the train's paper napkin supply."

"You don't write on a tablet?"

"I prefer the old pen-to-paper technique. Something about the tactile nature of it sparks my creativity in a way typing on a device never does. Or, at least, it used to." He returned the book to his bag, took a breath, and settled his gaze on the park across the street. "Now, what can we learn about Christmas from this town?"

"Well..." She did a slow twirl to take in the view. "There are decorations."

"What kind? Moore writes, 'Visions of sugar plumbs,' not just 'plums.' He's specific and that changes the meaning. A plumb is a piece of fruit; a sugar plumb is a candy."

As they stood there, surveying the town, Paige noticed something sticking out of Davyn's bag.

"What's that sheet of paper?"

"Hmm. The cashier must have stuffed it in there. Probably an ad of some kind."

When he passed it to her, she unfolded it and read the title. "Your Pinecone Christmas Bucket List."

"Perfect. We'll do all the things on the list and really get into the Christmas spirit."

Paige scanned the entries. "There're seventy-five activities. We'll never get them all done before dark."

"We won't get to any of them if we don't start now." He rested a hand on her shoulder, calming her nerves. "We can do this. Trust me."

And, for some reason, she did.

The flip side of the paper had a map of the town, the locations of all the activities clearly marked. Davyn checked the street names at the intersection and figured out where they were. "The closest activity to us is number twenty-eight."

Paige compared the number to the list. "That's 'Roast chestnuts on an open fire.'"

"It's just down the street. This way."

He took her hand and led her past a flower shop and a busy toy store. Her nose led her the rest of the way.

Between two businesses—one that sold crafts and another that served takeout food—was a vacant lot where a short, thin man stood tending a fire. He held a rectangular mesh metal box in the flames, the box's long handle keeping his fingers safe.

"I've already washed and scored the chestnuts," he explained to the gathering crowd. "They've been roasting for fifteen minutes, so another five should do them. Here, have a try."

He offered the roaster to Paige, and she held it over the fire, as instructed. The metal lid allowed her to shake the chestnuts around without any of them falling out.

"You score them?" she asked.

"Makes them easier to peel later. You might miss the popping noise, though. And sometimes, the explosions."

One chestnut gave a little pop, on cue, and the crowd laughed.

"I have some here I've already peeled and rubbed with butter and cinnamon." The man handed everyone their own paper cone filled with the fragrant nuts that made snapping and crackling sounds as they cooled. They tasted sweet and nutty with a hint of the wood fire.

"What's the next place on our map?" she asked Davyn.

"Don't go running off now," the thin man advised, as he began roasting a new batch of nuts. "The parade is about to begin."

Chapter Eight

The number and quality of the parade's entries impressed Davyn. Especially for a small town. Nothing as theatrical as the annual Hollywood Christmas Parade, of course. It was better somehow. Original. Along with the expected high school marching band, there were cowboys on horses, suede-clad gents walking while twirling lassoes, tuxedoed chauffeurs driving antique cars, firefighters walking alongside a firetruck decorated with Christmas lights, and a farm tractor pulling a ukelele group that sang and played, *Feliz Navidad*.

While he and Paige watched the floats go by, they munched on their shared bag of chestnuts. When their hands brushed, a zing coursed through Davyn that reminded him of his teenage years and the heady rush that came from a first crush.

The next entry recreated the nativity scene. There was Mary, a swathed bundle in her arms, Joseph, three Wise Men, a couple of angels, a live donkey and several lambs. The image made Davyn remember his Sunday school lessons and how Jesus inspired the traditional Christmas colors of green, red, and gold.

Green represented eternal life, like the pines that surrounded the town, which didn't lose their leaves in winter. Red symbolized the blood Christ shed for mankind during the crucifixion. And gold, traditionally associated with royalty, was one of the three gifts brought by the Magi.

"Gold, frankincense, and myrrh," he mused aloud.

"What is frankincense?"

"A resin, I believe. It's used to make perfumes and incense."

"Makes sense."

"Da-dum-dum."

Her brows rose, as if she were a little surprised by the pun herself, and then she asked, "What about myrrh?"

"I think it's used in medicines."

She tipped her head to one side with a cocky flair. "So, it's *myrrh-dicinal*?"

"Very good." She might be self-conscious about failing high school English, but Paige caught on fast, producing an impressive wordplay. He clapped his hands in appreciation, and she curtsied in response. "One more pun and you win the prize."

"*Myrrh-velous*." She looked up at him, her cheeks pink from the cold, her lips red and glistening. "So, what's the prize?"

He longed for a stolen kiss, but felt it was too soon in their relationship for him to act on it. And there were too many people around. He preferred to wait, find the right moment, and kiss her thoroughly. He settled for wrapping an arm around her waist, and his heart kicked against his ribs when she snuggled closer.

Santa took that moment to make his appearance, seated in a throne-like chair, Mrs. Claus at his side. Roller skating elves with buckets of candy canes handed out their treats to the kids lining the sidewalk. The children's shrieks of glee almost drowned out the float's taped music *Santa Claus is Coming to Town*.

Parade over, Davyn checked his watch. "It's past noon. Did you want to get some lunch?"

She patted her stomach. "I'm full from the chestnuts."

"Me too." Although he wouldn't mind a coffee or some hot chocolate to chase them down. He consulted their Christmas Bucket List. Their next stop would bring him the very thing he craved. "On to our housing project."

Paige soon discovered what Davyn meant when they ended up on the doorstep of the local bakery. "We're going to make a gingerbread house?"

"That's the plan."

The owners had divided the bakery into stations. Paige and Davyn, armed with cups of hot chocolate, started at the dough-making table and observed how the bakers combined flour, baking soda, and spices with shortening, sugar, and molasses. Though this heavy dough wasn't ideal for eating, it smelled delicious—rich and spicy.

At the next station, the baker rolled out the dough and cut windows and doors into the slabs of gingerbread, before sliding it into the oven.

Finally, at the last station, they discovered how to melt colored candies in the window spaces to create a stained-glass effect. From there, they could construct their own gingerbread house.

They worked together, Davyn holding the cake walls in place, while Paige, armed with the piping bag, applied frosting to secure the joins.

She noticed several of the train passengers also taking part. Davyn must have recognized them too because he was soon asking her, "Ever wonder who's behind this trip? This contest? Ever wonder who would have the money and resources to pull it off?"

"You mean it isn't you?"

He chuckled. "I wish."

"Actually," she whispered, "I kind of wonder about those two. The middle-aged couple who always dress alike." Paige pointed her nose at the pair, who were at another table, both wearing Santa hats. The man playfully squirted his missus with icing.

"Why do you suspect them?"

"Well, they always seem to be around whenever anything happens. And they seem to have an endless supply of matching outfits. That says money to me, and whoever's behind all this has got to have great gobs of money."

"'Great Gobs of Money?' Isn't that an old Jerry Lee Lewis song?"

Paige suppressed a laugh and elbowed him in the ribs. "Seriously, now. Who do you think our benefactor is? Any guesses?"

"What makes you think they're on the train? They're probably sitting in a penthouse overlooking a sandy beach, with the air conditioning turned up high."

"Really? Wouldn't they want to be a part of this? To see what happens?"

Their conversation stopped while they concentrated on adding the roof to the house. Installation complete, Davyn continued.

"If I had to guess who our benefactor is, I'd pick Jenny."

"An interesting choice. Why her?"

"She's the front person, the one who orchestrates everything."

"Going for the obvious, huh, Columbo?"

"Naturally, Matlock. I'm betting on the person hiding in plain sight."

Once everyone had their gingerbread houses assembled, the baker explained how to decorate them. With icing, Paige set out to make icicles on the eves, but her hand proved unsteady. She thrust the piping bag at Davyn. "Here, you do it."

"I'll help." He took her hands in his and guided her with the delicate work.

She liked the feel of his hands on hers, and didn't want him to let go. But his touch distracted her from the task so much that the icicles ended up looking more like the heavy decorative molding one might find on a German alpine house. They soon ran out of icing and finished by adding candy accents until they were both satisfied with their creation.

Hungry after all their efforts, they split one of the pre-made sandwiches the bakery sold—roasted turkey with gouda cheese, arugula, and apple on sourdough bread. For dessert, the owners gave all the gingerbread house builders a gingerbread cookie.

"Time to work off our snack with an activity," Paige announced.

Davyn handed her the map. "I picked this one. You pick the next."

She ran her index finger over the suggestions on their Christmas Bucket List, stopping a third of the way down the first column.

"I know the perfect thing." She waggled her brows. "Are you ready to shoot the duck?"

Chapter Nine

S kating on the town's open-air rink was number twelve on the
Christmas Bucket List. They could have looked for used skates
at the thrift store, but Paige took the chance that some enterprising
businessperson would rent skates at the site.

And she was right.

A couple of ginger-headed teenagers—a brother and sister, judging by the way they teased each other—rented skates and helmets
out of an old, gutted, camping trailer filled with shelving. They'd
also rigged their makeshift store with a sound system that played
Christmas tunes. All country, of course.

"What size do you take?" Paige asked Davyn.

"I haven't got a clue. I've never been on skates in my life."

"And I've never written a poem. It'll be a day of firsts for both of us."

After selecting their skates and paying their rental fees, they followed the wide paved trail, which encircled the rink and led back to a parking lot. Families with strollers and folks with mobility issues moseyed along it, enjoying the scenery.

The sun was beginning its fast dip toward twilight, but the area had lampposts around the perimeter for illumination. And, since the train wasn't leaving until after supper, she and Davyn had lots of time.

About two dozen skaters were already on the ice, which was the size of a standard hockey rink. Several couples glided hand in hand, but mostly lone individuals practiced spins, jumps, and hockey stops. Beyond them, workers on ladders decorated a huge pine—a twenty-footer, at least.

The smoky scent of hot dogs filled the air. Paige saw a woman selling them from a booth on the opposite side of the rink. And, true to form, that middle-aged couple with the matching Santa hats were standing in the long line to buy a tasty meal.

Paige pointed them out to Davyn. "Think they followed us here?"

She also spotted Dalton Wainwright. She'd first met the attractive brown-eyed, brown-haired man when they boarded the train. Dal was easily recognizable because everyone remembered his scruffy companion. Restrained on a leash, the pup sniffed at the ground.

"I think that guy has the cabin next to mine," Davyn said. "I've heard his dog yip a few times."

"That's Grace. She's a Brussels...uh...something or other." The small, reddish-brown dog had an amazing amount of facial hair. "I think she looks like a cute George Armstrong Custer. Except for her stubby tail and torn ear."

"Perhaps she's part Vincent van Gogh."

Paige laughed and headed for one of the many benches dotting the edge of the rink. They sat, and she showed Davyn how to tie his laces. On the short walk to the ice, she spied two more train passengers—the elderly, wheelchair user, Mr. Watson, and his nurse Maddie. Luckily, a medic was nearby tonight if anyone got hurt.

"At an indoor rink, you'd be able to hold on to the barrier," she told Davyn.

"For now, how about some training wheels?"

"That's where I come in." She stretched out her hand to him. "Just hold on to me, and I'll support you."

"Support me? I must outweigh you by fifty pounds."

She took a moment to admire the distribution. For a guy whose work involved sitting at a desk pushing a pen, he had an athletic build—lean and toned. She shook her head to clear it and went on with the lesson.

"We'll step onto the ice carefully. Try to keep your ankles straight."

Once on the rink, she gave him a minute to get used to the feel of the skates. "Now, you're going to march. Bend your knees a little. That'll help you keep your balance."

"What if I fall?"

Wasn't that a Keith Urban lyric? "Falling is a given. Everyone falls. But I'll show you how to get on your feet again."

She held his hands and skated backward while he moved forward. "Don't watch your feet. Keep your head up."

"That's easy...if I get to look at you."

Despite the cold, her cheeks warmed. He was easy to look at too, with his California tan, those hazel eyes, and that thick mess of dark hair that was *oh, so touchable*. She forced herself to be content with holding onto his hands. That contact was more than enough to make her stomach do a flip-flop.

"Now, put your feet together and glide," she instructed and led him around the rink twice. "You're doing great."

But he was still a little tight-limbed. She needed to distract him, to loosen him up. She could sing along with Dan + Shay's *Take Me Home for Christmas* but doubted her ability to stay on pitch. Conversation might do the trick.

"Why are you here?" she asked him.

"Skating with you?"

"I mean, why did you enter the contest?"

He shrugged and threw himself off balance, but she held on tight. "A change of scenery," he answered, once he'd found his footing. "Some time to think about my next steps. What I'll do with my life now."

"If you win the grand prize, will you publish another book?"

"With the money? No. I want to start a legal aid fund for artists accused like I was. How about you?"

Could she be honest with him? Open herself up? "I'd like to help kids who..." She finished her sentence, glancing over her shoulder to make sure no one was behind her.

"Pardon? I missed that."

Darn. She didn't want to say it again. Still, sometimes it was easier to talk to a stranger than someone you knew. At the diner, she'd listened to hundreds of folks share their secrets. Chatty people just passing through knew their confessions were safe with her because they'd never see her again.

Just like Davyn. Would she ever see him after this trip?

"I said *stutter*."

Her admission met with silence. Did he think her cause was stupid?

"I had a classmate in third grade who stuttered," he said at last, easing her tension. "I wonder what percentage of kids do."

"About five percent worldwide. Three-quarters of them will overcome it by adulthood."

"Sounds like you've done your research."

"Yes, when I originally entered the contest for the train trip. Our benefactor must have thought it was a worthy cause too, since I'm here."

"I think anything that benefits children is worthwhile. But how did you get interested in the condition? Did you know a kid who stuttered?"

Did she ever. A person she saw every day. Someone she couldn't escape. That stutterer's image was in the mirror when she brushed her teeth in the morning, and when she pulled the covered elastic from her hair each night.

"Yes. Me. I was that kid."

"You stuttered?"

"Still do. Sometimes." When they'd met at breakfast, she'd tripped over her Cs and Ms. If he hadn't noticed, maybe all the therapy she'd done as a child had paid off.

"I want to help other kids, like me, who have Childhood-Onset Fluency Disorder. Or COFD." And suffered at the hands of bullies because of it. "At elementary school, the kids called me Miss Stutter from Wamsutter."

"Kids can be cruel."

"Yes." And the taunts only got worse following an incident she'd rather forget. Years later, after the humiliation of stammering through a high school presentation, she'd quit mid-semester, never to return.

"How do you treat stuttering?"

"There are several techniques," she explained. "Slowing my speech helps. My stammer returns in times of stress, though."

"I hadn't noticed."

Was he being honest? Or kind? Either way, she thanked him.

"Thank me by keeping your promise," he replied.

"My promise?"

"Yes, teacher. You said something about ducks."

"Shoot-the-duck. I'll show you." She slowed their speed. "Now, I'm going to let go of your hands. Remember to keep your knees bent. If you feel unsteady, hold your arms out to find your balance and, if you still think you're going to fall, grab your knees. If all else fails and you can't stay upright, try to fall backward onto your butt."

"The cushy part. Got it."

"If ever you start moving and need to stop, drag a foot."

"Will do."

She gradually released her hold on him. Confident he could remain on his feet, she stepped back. "One shoot-the-duck, coming up."

Paige skated ahead, avoiding the others on the rink, and worked up speed as she doubled back toward him. She crouched down, then extended one leg and grabbed her foot.

Davyn applauded and lost his balance. He tried all the tricks she'd given him and finished by windmilling his arms. She reached him in time to help break his fall. They were so close that the mist from their breaths mingled in the cold air.

Close enough to kiss.

Get over yourself, Paige Chamberlain. He wasn't even thinking of kissing her. No matter how much she might want him to try.

"Are you okay?" she asked, sobering.

"Yeah...I think." He groaned, then chuckled, assuring her he was fine.

"See? Falling isn't so bad. Now, I'll show you how to get on your feet again." *Good, Paige. Go back to the business at hand and stop thinking about his lips.* "First, get on your hands and knees. Next, raise one knee and place the skate of that foot on the ice." She illustrated how to do it, and he repeated the moves.

"Great. Now, put your weight on that leg. Brace your hands on your bent leg to help you up, if you need it, and come to a standing position."

He did and clutched her arms for balance. Or was there another reason he held her so close?

"Ten...nine...eight..."

One voice started the countdown, and soon others joined in. It took Paige a moment to realize the chanting had nothing to do with her hopes of a kiss, and everything to do with the lighting of the tree.

"Four...three...two...one!"

A thousand tiny lights—blue, red, green, yellow, white, and purple—lit up the tree, turning it into a magical beacon against the blackening night. At the very top, a multi-pointed star sparkled as bright as any in the dark sky. The crowd clapped, drowning out *On This Winter's Night* by Lady A.

"Feels like New Year's Eve," Davyn said, his voice husky. He leaned in, as if he might kiss her, and she closed her eyes, wanting to feel his lips on hers more than anything.

"Help!" someone cried.

The sharpness of the raised voice broke Paige and Davyn apart. Across the rink, the female half of the couple with the matching outfits dropped the hotdog she'd been holding and brought her hands to her throat.

"She's choking!" her male companion yelled. *"Help!"*

The man flailed his arms to get the attention of the nurse on the other side of the rink. The way Davyn figured it, Maddie would never reach them in time on foot. And, on skates, he'd take even longer.

A second later, Paige shot away from him and sped across the ice. Once there, she slipped in behind the choking victim, wrapped her arms around the woman's middle, and thrust her clenched fists inward and upward.

Once. Twice. Three times.

A chunk of hotdog popped out of the woman's mouth and into the snow. The little dog yipped and made a beeline for the discarded fragment. Her owner, Dal, intercepted her before she could reach the scrap, picked her up, and gave her a light chastisement.

"No, Grace. That's not for you."

Maddie finally arrived at the woman's side and checked that she was okay. When Paige returned to Davyn, he wrapped his arms around her.

"You're a hero. I mean, a heroine."

She blushed. "Hardly."

"You are. You just saved that woman." He'd lost a kiss over it, of course, but he'd look for another opportunity to recapture the magic of the moment. "Where did you learn to do that?"

"The Heimlich maneuver comes in handy when you're a waitress. I mean, server. I did what anyone would have."

"Everyone else was standing around—me included. Not everyone would know what to do."

He gave her another squeeze. And, since she seemed in no hurry to move, he held on.

Davyn buried his nose in the sweet floral scent of her hair and relished the way her body fit against his. He kissed her temple, then whispered in her ear, putting every ounce of pride he felt for her into his words.

"You did."

Chapter Ten

T hey raced back to the train, dropped their coats in Davyn's cabin, and headed to their assigned dining car. Over supper, they pulled out their notebooks and Davyn actually picked up a pen!

It felt awkward in his hand, foreign. Like when he was a kid, coming back to school in September, after spending the entire summer fishing and playing football.

They scribbled in their notebooks, discussing and recording all their thoughts about the day at a frenetic speed. They captured their impressions of the popping chestnuts, the nativity scene, the elves on roller skates, and the lighting of the tree. Davyn emphasized how Christmas was a time for kindness, a time to help one another, just as Paige had helped the couple with the matching Santa hats. They recorded it all—the sounds, the colors, the scents, the tastes, and the feel of the cold against their cheeks.

Once back in Davyn's cabin, they began the poem, writing on sheets of foolscap in a flurry. They compared notes, suggested ideas, and consulted Paige's rhyming dictionary; a resource Davyn had seldom used before.

Nor had he ever collaborated until this moment. Had never dabbled with this kind of give and take. Neither of them assumed the role of leader. They journeyed through the words together, one often completing the other's line.

Within half an hour, they had the skeleton of their poem complete. At the end of two, they had a polished work.

They whooped, they laughed, they hugged, then whooped again, the little dog next door punctuating their exuberance with a yowl.

Davyn popped the loose pages of their creation into the manila folder on his desk and rubbed his palms together. "Time to celebrate."

"Champagne?" Paige suggested.

"Why not?"

She pushed herself up from the desk chair, but he motioned for her to stay. "I'll grab a bottle and glasses from the bartender and be right back."

If he was lucky, he might earn a congratulatory kiss too.

With Davyn gone, Paige returned to the manila folder and reread their creation.

She grabbed her pen again and recorded their poem in her notebook, so she'd have her own copy of the work she'd composed with the famous Davyn Kayne.

As she jotted down the words, her heart beat a little faster. She'd never written anything this good in her entire life. Never would have thought it possible.

But Davyn believed in her and had showed her she could do it. He'd treated her like an equal who had something special to contribute. She'd never be able to thank him enough.

But why had the contest organizers partnered them together? Surely other contestants on board had more writing experience than her.

Their mysterious benefactor appeared to possess a knowledge of their backgrounds and had assigned them the challenge of overcoming their past wounds. For Paige, that involved her failure of tenth grade English. For Davyn, it challenged his poetic output. And he'd risen to the occasion, judging by the number of other pages in the file.

When she replaced the sheet of foolscap in the folder, several other pages of verse slipped out and scattered across the floor.

Darn.

She hoped he'd numbered them, otherwise she'd never get them back in the right order.

She sank to her knees and picked up the closest one, but couldn't find a page number. And, oddly, someone had typed the poem. Hadn't Davyn said he preferred to use pen to paper?

She grabbed another page. A handwritten one. With her and Davyn jotting down ideas, she'd become familiar with his penmanship.

Someone else wrote this poem.

She checked all the extra pages. The only trace of Davyn's input was a few scribbled notes in red ink.

A chill crept through her, from the inside out, and she hugged herself for warmth.

What had Davyn said when she'd asked about the plagiarism accusations against him? *That some people found themselves charged with lots of things they hadn't done.*

A non-answer. One that didn't address the question. He didn't admit the charge was true. But he hadn't denied it, either.

The sound of clinking glass made her look up. Davyn stood in the open doorway, a mini bottle of champagne in one hand and two fluted glasses in the other.

He took in the scattered papers on the floor. "What happened?"

Everything. She'd believed in him. Thought he'd believed in her. But he was a liar. A fake. And she wanted to hear him admit it.

She scooped up a handful of the poems, stood, and faced him. "Why did you stop writing?"

A line appeared between his brows. "You know why."

"Because you got caught plagiarizing?" She thrust the pages at him as proof. It was up to him to set the record straight. To either admit or deny it.

He stiffened. His face drained of color. "Is that what you think?"

"What else can I think when you won't answer the question?" Paige flung the poems at him, hoping for any kind of reaction.

He didn't catch the pages. Just let them flutter about him to the floor like giant flakes of snow.

He stepped through them, set the unopened champagne and the glasses on top of the minibar, then turned on his heel, and strode away.

Chapter Eleven

After waiting fifteen minutes, Paige declared Davyn MIA. He intended to leave her question unanswered.

She picked up her coat and her notebook. Her personal relationship with Davyn might be over, but she still hoped to win the competition. Thankfully, she'd had the forethought to make that copy of their poem—hard proof she'd completed her task.

She retreated to her cabin but couldn't stay there. Still shaky from the confrontation with Davyn, she needed a distraction. Though she wasn't much of a drinker, she found herself in the bar car. At least Bruce would provide a sympathetic ear.

The jazz trio was playing their usual closing number, *Feeling Good*, while Paige was feeling anything but. Alanis Morissette might have described that as ironic but, after reviewing the glossary of terms in her rhyming dictionary, Paige now knew better.

When the bassist and clarinetist packed up for the night, the pianist, Jamila Scott, continued to run her long, graceful fingers over the keys. With short curls framing her lovely face, she could have passed for Naomie Harris's Moneypenny—could have been the stunt double for that shaving scene with Daniel Craig. Tonight, she wore a deep purple, floor-length gown, with silver metallic threads running through the material. *Magnificent.*

Paige ordered a glass of Pinot Grigio from Bruce and turned to find a seat. That's when she noticed the only other patron. The pretty woman had long, chocolate-colored hair—a far cry from Paige's drab, mousy brown.

The woman smiled and gestured for Paige to take the seat opposite her. "It seems silly for us to sit at different tables. I'm Tess Barton."

Paige had seen her around the train, but they hadn't formally met. "Paige Chamberlain." After they shook hands, she took the offered seat.

"Come here often?" Tess asked.

"Yes. I like to get together with some of the train staff after their shifts. I'm a server myself." Darned if Davyn's politically correct term hadn't invaded her speech. "You?"

"I come for the music."

Seeming to take that as her cue, Jamila glanced over her shoulder at them and grinned. She turned back to the piano and, at full volume, began singing about a soldier and his sweetheart. After the first verse, she launched into the chorus, her voice playful.

K-K-K-Katy, beautiful Katy,
You're the only g-g-g-girl that I adore.
When the m-m-m-moon shines over the cowshed,

I'll be waiting at the k-k-k-kitchen door.

Heat blazed across Paige's cheeks. Had the singer intentionally planned to mock her?

"What the heck kind of song is that?" She slapped a hand over her mouth. Hadn't meant to say that out loud and hoped Jamila hadn't overheard.

"It's a World War I song," Tess told her. "I only know because my great-grandfather used to sing it. You see, the soldier is so nervous about meeting his sweetheart, he stutters."

"I noticed." Paige clutched her wineglass tighter.

"Funny, huh?

"Hilarious."

Tess took a sip of her drink—straight up ginger ale, from the looks of it. "Enjoying the trip?"

"Yes." Until she'd found those pages in Davyn's room. That and Jamila's song had put her on edge. "Mostly." She rolled her shoulders and tipped back her wine.

"Me too. Mostly."

"You don't have a partner yet?"

"Interesting you put it like that. I'd planned to be here with the man I was seeing. We entered the contest together."

"He didn't come along?"

"We broke up."

It seemed rude to ask why, but Paige was curious, so she kept her mouth shut, hoping Tess would explain.

"Let's just say we were ill-matched. I work with a kennel, and he hates dogs. And there were other problems..."

Tess took a breath, as if to continue, but then waved her hand, shooing the thought away. "I should head back to my cabin. Make an early night of it." She finished her drink and rose from her seat. "Pleasant dreams."

"Good night." Paige watched her go. Apparently, if she was going to learn more about Tess's past, she'd have to wait.

When Jamila started playing Lady Gaga's *Poker Face*, with all those stuttering p-p-ps, Paige left her wine unfinished and walked out of the bar car.

Chapter Twelve

Paige dragged her feet back to her cabin, ready to pack it in for the night. She shut the window shade and pulled the covered elastic from her hair.

Out of her peripheral vision, she caught movement—a note sliding under her door.

Was it from Davyn?

She rushed to the door, opened it, and stared into space. She looked to her right down the long corridor.

No one. Nothing.

She looked left. There, at the far end of the cabins, a figure opened the gangway door that connected this car to the next. Paige glimpsed a flash of purple and silver before the figure slipped through the door and disappeared.

Jamila Scott? Had the pianist delivered the note?

Paige picked it up and sat on her bed. She unfolded the paper to find a brief newspaper article, the kind of filler that appeared on a back page.

The last word on Davyn Kayne

Two years ago, newcomer Trig Hamish accused Kayne of plagiarism. Today, after an extensive investigation and trial, the courts fully exonerated Kayne, and fined Hamish $50,000 for his fraudulent submissions and ordered him to pay a portion of Kayne's court costs. In a recent interview, Kayne, free of his signature beard, said he'd found interim work in a mentorship position at his old alma mater. He is editing an anthology of his students' poems that will be out next spring. He has no immediate writing plans of his own.

Paige let the article fall to her side.

Exonerated? She'd missed that info when she'd first researched Davyn. And no wonder. After the juicy headlines condemning him, only this small article revealed the truth.

Were the poems she'd discovered in Davyn's compartment written by his students? Were the markings she found on them his edits for the anthology?

Paige's stomach took a slow dive to her shoes. She had to find Davyn. Had to apologize.

She ran to his cabin and knocked—*pounded*—while the little dog next door yipped. A woman from down the corridor, her white hair bound with curlers, poked her nose out of her cabin and cursed under her breath.

Paige apologized for the disturbance and checked the observation car next. But Davyn wasn't there either.

She tore around the train searching for him—her skin feverish, her mind whirling. How could he have slipped past her? Had he disembarked? Jumped off? Or was he hiding in his cabin, refusing to open the door?

Maybe hiding was a theme in his life. Maybe shaving off the beard he'd sported on his book cover was a way to avoid the public by disguising himself in plain sight.

The thought also led Paige to wonder about the figure she'd seen disappear into the neighboring car. Was it Jamila Scott? She'd played those stammering songs in the bar. Were they aimed directly at Paige? Like the note under her door?

It was curious that the musician seemed to know so much personal information. Could she be the one financing the trip? The one behind the contest?

The one who'd paired Paige with Davyn in the first place?

After spending some time on the rear open-air platform clearing his head, Davyn returned to his cabin. He pulled out his notebook and re-read the poem—the first he'd written in two years. Pride swelled in his chest, then something else ripped into him.

Heartache.

He caressed the pages, then tore them out of the notebook, ripped them into little bits, and flushed them down the toilet.

A knock sounded on his door. When he opened it, Paige stood there panting, her cheeks flushed.

"Back for round two? I think you said more than enough the first time." He grabbed the door handle and slid it to the right, but Paige shoved her foot on the track, blocking him from closing it.

"And I was wrong. There was this note...a news article..." She squeezed her eyes shut for a few seconds, took a breath, then began again.

"How I discovered the truth doesn't matter. Now, I know some-one falsely accused you."

She reached out as if she might touch him, but then pulled back. "If you didn't plagiarize another person's work, why did you just stand there when I confronted you? Why didn't you say some-thing?"

He'd spent the last year weighed down by disapproval and rejec-tion. Some days, he'd struggled to get out of bed. Then he'd met her, and that weight lifted. They'd joked together, had fun together, and created a satisfying piece of work together. He'd looked forward to spending the rest of the trip with her. To stay in touch once it ended.

Until she'd doubted him. That's when all that weight came crashing back, crushing him once again.

"What could I have said? You'd decided."

"And I'm sorry. Sorrier than I've ever been before in my life. I'm asking you to forgive me."

Davyn stared at her. The public had convicted and sentenced him ahead of the facts too. But damned if he hadn't expected more from Paige.

Before he could respond, Jenny appeared at his door.

"I'm so glad I found you together," their hostess said. "Tomorrow, we'll be stopping in Last Chance, Wyoming—aptly named as it was, and still is, the last chance for travelers to get fuel and provisions before reaching Montana."

She consulted the gold pendant watch she wore on a chain around her neck. "Goodness, is that the time? I guess we'll be stopping today. We've booked the Liberty Lights Auditorium there for the afternoon performance."

Davyn did a double take. Had he heard her correctly? "Performance?"

"Of your poem. It's all written and ready to go, I presume."

"Yes, but..." Paige's lips trembled. "...who said anything about perform-m-m-ming it?"

"Oh, I'm sure I mentioned that. The show is a fundraiser for the local food bank. Your joint task is to write and recite." Jenny giggled. "See that? I made a rhyme, myself. Now, you two better get some rest so you're bright-eyed for the show. I understand our mystery benefactor has invited the media and a few special guests from the publishing industry. So exciting!" She departed humming, *Have a Holly Jolly Christmas.*

But Davyn didn't feel so jolly, and Paige looked stricken. He took her by the arm and sat her down on his bed. "We need to talk."

Thankfully, a trained nurse was on board. Judging from Paige's pale cheeks and clammy skin, she just might faint.

Chapter Thirteen

Paige gulped. "I c-c-can't do it. Words like C-C-Christmas and m-m-merry...I c-c-can't say them in front of an audience."

"Yesterday, I saw you save someone from choking." Davyn shut his cabin door, then leaned against it. "You're a brave woman. You can do anything."

Sweet of him to say so, especially after she'd doubted him, but that didn't make it true.

"You don't understand. For m-m-my third grade Christmas Pageant, I had one line. I couldn't get it out of my m-m-mouth. Years later, in high school, I had to give a presentation, and the same thing happened. I'm a failure at public speaking."

"You're in good company then." Davyn remained by the door. He hadn't accepted her apology yet. Maybe he wouldn't. Maybe the level of closeness they'd shared yesterday was gone forever.

"I once heard an interview with Marilyn Monroe," he continued. "She confessed to having a stutter as a child—a stutter which recurred whenever she was nervous. She turned out to be one of the most glamorous, memorable stars that ever lived and, though self-educated, anything but a dumb blonde."

"Really?" He must still care to make such an effort to reassure her with this story. Or was he only concerned about the grand prize?

"Really," he replied. "I'd once thought to write lyrics about her but knew I couldn't beat Bernie Taupin and Elton John's collaboration."

He opened the minibar and retrieved a bottle of water. "Take a few minutes, relax, then we'll rehearse. The more comfortable we feel with the piece, the better we'll perform it."

He handed the drink to her. "It's okay to be nervous, Paige. I'm nervous too."

With his golden trophies, she assumed he'd be comfortable appearing in front of a crowd. But she doubted he'd imagined the crowd would include reporters and guests from the publishing business.

He returned to the bar, his back to her. "I didn't tell you earlier, but I've been suffering from a condition for a long time—a condition I never believed in before. Writer's block."

He let out a huff of breath that could have almost passed as a laugh if it hadn't sounded so forlorn. "I guess it stemmed from the initial accusation of plagiarism and only grew during the court case. Writing—something I'd once loved to do—became a struggle. I did it less and less until...one day...I realized I hadn't written in months. And I was afraid to start again. Intellectually, I knew I hadn't plagiarized my accuser but, everywhere I went, people were talking about my guilt so much, I second-guessed myself. I worried that all my ideas were really someone else's. That I'd inadvertently copy another writer's words."

He faced her. "Yes, Paige. I am very nervous about reciting our poem in front of an audience—an audience that includes members from my industry and the press. They'll be judging me far more than they'll be judging you."

She heard the raw truth in his voice—the hurt, the dread. If she messed up the poem, people might mock her for a day or two, but it could haunt Davyn forever. His career hung in the balance yet again. Offering him moral support was the least she could do.

They rehearsed the piece—the strain between them adding to her nerves. Yes, he'd shown her kindness by trying to calm her fears, by giving her the water, by leading her to a seat in his cabin, but he hadn't touched her since. Hadn't joked with her like before. And no matter how many times they went over the piece, she couldn't get through it without stumbling.

"You should recite the poem on your own. Without me."

Davyn shook his head. "This is a joint task, remember? We're a team. We're in this together. Those are the rules."

Paige sighed and read her part over again, the lines blurring. She rubbed her eyes. Good thing she'd almost memorized the piece. If only she could get the words in her brain to come out of her mouth.

"Try slowing down," Davyn suggested. "You told me that helped."

"If I talk any slower, I'll put the audience to sleep."

"That's something we could both use."

She saw the dark smudges under his eyes. It was past three in the morning, and her anxiety was keeping him awake and increasing his stress. "I'll go to my cabin."

She stood, but he waved her back down. "You don't have to leave." He pulled the comforter over her legs.

"What about you?"

"I'll take the chair."

Not fair, but he insisted. She curled up on her side. Though her eyes burned with fatigue, the chug-chug of the train provided a comforting white noise, and the motion made her feel like a baby in a cradle.

When she opened her eyes again, daylight peeked through the window blind. Davyn emerged from the washroom, shaved and handsome in his customary dark pants, paired with a royal blue dress shirt and black tie.

"Sorry. I must have dozed off when I should have been going over the poem. Why didn't you wake me?"

"You needed rest more than rehearsal time. While you napped, I found something that will reassure you." He held up his phone. "I Googled the performance venue. It holds only fifty seats. Even if we make a flub, few people will see it or even care."

Her shoulders relaxed and her stomach settled until she thought about what he'd said. Did he *expect* them to mess up?

And what about the media? And those invited publishers? She didn't want to make Davyn look bad in front of them.

Jitters back, she returned to her cabin, showered and changed into something nicer—a black skirt and a blue top with a crocheted white collar that looked like icicles. If nothing else, she and Davyn would have color-coordinated outfits.

The train pulled into Last Chance's station and a shuttle bus drove them, and the other teams, to the auditorium, then the organizers herded them onto the stage. A heavy red velvet curtain separated Paige and Davyn from the murmuring audience on the other side.

Jenny, her voice hushed, reminded the contestants that the show would benefit the local food bank. Then she consulted her clipboard and explained the line-up to everyone involved.

"The Team Stirs are on first. They'll be showing a PowerPoint presentation on how they created the world's largest sticky toffee pudding. Afterward, it will be the Mama Mias with their game, then a short musical interlude. Following that, Davyn and Paige are on."

Paige wished they could go on first and be done with it. Appearing last meant she'd be anxious and tense throughout the entire show. Davyn felt the same, judging by the beads of sweat on his forehead.

"Our stage manager is Sid," Jenny went on. She gestured to a wiry, balding man wearing black clothes and a headset. "He'll cue you."

Jenny adjusted her Mrs. Claus glasses on her nose and flashed a toothy grin. "Sid will be around with a release form for you to sign. Do your best to ignore the cameras and, as they say in the theater...break a leg!" Jenny strode off, the other two teams trailing behind her.

Did she say cameras? Paige and Davyn exchanged a panicked look.

He approached Sid. "Excuse me. Is this being filmed?"

"For viewers across Wyoming," the stage manager replied. "A potential 600,000 people."

Paige didn't mean to moan out loud, but it beat crying. She was about to be humiliated in front of her neighbors, her customers, her people.

"Don't worry." Davyn rested his hands on her shoulders. "These kinds of TV appearances are always taped and edited. If we mess up, we'll just start over."

At least, that was a little reassuring.

"Oh, no," Sid interjected. "We're broadcasting this show live." He thrust a pen and a form at her. "Sign here."

"Do we have to?" Her throat constricted, her question pitched higher, making her sound like a boy soprano.

Sid sighed. "Only if you want a shot at the twenty-five grand."

Paige nudged Davyn and whispered, "C-c-can they do that? Should we c-c-consult a lawyer?"

"The way I figure it, everyone today has cell phones. Anyone in the audience could film us, upload it to YouTube, and have it go viral." Davyn took the pen and the form. "We might as well sign and get it over with."

He did, then passed the pen to Paige. But her hand was shaking so hard, she dropped the pen on the floor.

While Sid retrieved it, Davyn caught her arm and drew her close. "Remember how well you kept your cool the morning you helped serve in the dining car? Your hands were steady the whole time. Today, instead of serving up food, you'll be serving up a poem. Much easier."

Could she do it and win the prize money? "So, I can help other kids who stutter?"

"Yes. And I need your help too, Paige. All those people in the audience think I stole someone else's words. Just like you did. I need to convince them otherwise. I need your support...like when we were skating."

Back when things were going so well between them. "I remember."

"I asked you what would happen if I fell. You said falling is inevitable, as in life. But you promised you'd help me get back on my feet again. Help me get back up now."

She owed him that. For the kids, the food bank, and for Davyn, she'd do it. "It'll be five minutes out of my life. I can stand anything for five minutes." She grasped the pen and signed—her hands cold, her body trembling.

Alongside Davyn, she watched from the wings, her knees threatening to give out, as the Team Stirs went on first. Their PowerPoint presentation was well-organized but overly long. Fortunately, they cracked a few jokes along the way to keep the audience's attention.

Then the Mama Mias took their turn. They appeared wearing helmets with reindeer antlers and received huge laughs over their getup. They explained that the helmets also had Velcro strips on them, as did the pile of presents onstage. With their hands behind their back and, using only their headgear, they picked up the packages and tossed them through the goal, which was a large wreath.

Following their short demo, they selected random kids from the audience to play the game. The rules were confusing. Or maybe Paige found it confusing because she was simultaneously running the poem's lines in her mind. Still, she could tell the game was a hit, with the spectators in hysterics at the kids' antics.

After the winner was announced, all the children returned to their seats with Lego sets as a thank-you for playing. The audience cheered, the curtains closed, and stagehands, dressed in black, ran about clearing the smashed packages and discarded helmets.

On the other side of the curtain, a piano banged out *Santa Claus is Coming to Town* and, at Jenny's urging, the audience sang along.

The stage manager told Paige and Davyn to stand ready, but how could they follow the Reindeer Toss? "You're on right after Jamila Scott," Sid told them.

Jamila? What was she doing here?

Davyn clasped Paige's hand. "You can do this. *We* can do this."

He led her to the center of the stage, behind the closed curtain. The pianist's distinctive voice floated through the sound system as she sang a ballad about a woman asking for unconditional l-l-l-l-l-l-l-love.

Seriously? How many of these stuttering songs did Jamila know?

At the end of the *number*, Jenny addressed the audience. "Jamila Scott, everyone."

As the applause faded, Jenny continued. "We included that song in today's program because we're all searching for unconditional love. Especially at this time of year. And it might surprise you but, Jamila has an entire repertoire of what we call stuttering songs—which are songs with a stutter built into the lyrics. Why did you pick one of these songs to perform now, Jamila?"

To introduce the stutterer behind the curtain. That's what Paige expected Jamila to answer. She closed her eyes, stiffened, and prepared for the cheap shot.

"Because I s-s-stutter," Jamila said.

Paige's eyes popped open, along with her mouth. *What?!*

"I used to be a lot worse, believe me," Jamila went on. "It made me feel s-s-stupid. But music really helped. I learned I could s-s-sing, without s-s-stuttering and I didn't feel s-s-so s-s-stupid anymore."

Jamila stuttered too?!

Paige replayed her memories. Till now, she'd only ever heard Jamila sing, not speak, so she didn't know the singer had the same problem. All this time, she'd thought Jamila was mocking her. But the song choices had nothing to do with Paige.

"If you s-s-stutter, you don't need to feel s-s-stupid either," Jamila advised the gathering. "It has nothing to do with intelligence. It just means you're unique. And that's okay."

Was it? After Jamila's speech, the audience might be more forgiving when Paige stuttered. Or would they think she was poking fun at the musician and boo?

"For our last act, we have Team Rhyme and Dine," Jenny announced, "whose members are Paige Chamberlain and Davyn Kayne. And they're going to recite an original Christmas poem."

The curtains opened and the stage lights blinded Paige. She heard scattered applause, then shuffling, and a cough.

A bitter sense of déjà vu hit her. Images from her Grade 3 Christmas Pageant flashed in her mind—the shadowed audience, the kids' giggles, the pressure to say her lines without stumbling...and failing.

Beside her, Davyn began. She was in such a fog she hardly recognized the words of their poem. He gave her hand a squeeze—her cue to speak. Knees shaking, she opened her mouth, unsure of what would come out.

Somehow, she formed words and repeated the lines of poetry they'd written. She recited her part about the roasting chestnuts and their 'symphony of cinnamon.' Her section on the frenetic energy of the roller skating elves, 'never strolling, always rock and rolling.' The way the colors of Christmas 'bedecked the night, with evergreens and crimsons bright.' The beauty and awe of the nativity's 'cradled dreams,' providing 'a glorious sight, on a frost-kissed night.' Together, after what felt like forever, they made it to the end of the piece.

And met with silence.

Was the poem she'd thought so imaginative a flop? Or had her delivery of it put the audience to sleep? Either way, Paige couldn't wait to exit the stage.

As she turned to run, the applause started. Davyn caught her arm, just as he had on the train when they'd first met face to face. A million years ago.

They stood there together as the applause built, from the sound of scattered raindrops to thunder.

Paige basked in it. Her chest swelled with pride and a tear trickled down her cheek. And when Davyn took her hand, her pulse jumped.

They bowed and bowed again. As the clapping subsided, Davyn held up his free hand to quiet the audience.

"There's one more poem I'd like to recite," he said. "A bonus piece of verse for you. It's the first I've written on my own in two years. Last night, after a moment of angst, I tore it up, but I rewrote it from memory this morning. And I dedicate it to my teammate, Paige Chamberlain."

Paige's hands fluttered to her cheeks. *To me?* After the way she'd treated him?

Davyn cleared his throat and nodded at Jamila, who began to play an accompaniment to his words.

Last Christmas, I was so blue.
Alone and lost. My life askew.
No friends to confide in. I had so few.
Christmas, for me, was through.
"I have no plans this Christmas."
That's what I'd always say.
I'd shrug and keep repeating,
"It's just another day."
I didn't wrap a present.
I didn't deck a hall.
I huddled in my darkened room,
Lamenting my downfall.
I had no plans this Christmas,
Until you came along.
Expected I'd be lonely,
You showed me I was wrong.
This Christmas, I start anew.
From broken pieces to something true.
You light up my world with all that you do.
That's why Christmas, for me, is you.

Paige's vision misted and blurred. The audience disappeared. Nothing mattered but Davyn, and the sweet poem he'd written.

From his heart to hers.

She was vaguely aware of balloons and confetti falling around them, and of the crowd's applause and whistles. But she was keenly aware of Davyn and how he leaned into her. How his lips felt against hers, and spread warmth through her, right to her toes.

Then people swarmed around them. Reporters appeared and shouted questions as they jostled for position. Fast-talking agents and publishers offered representation. The horde split her and Davyn apart and then swept him away.

And Paige remained standing there, onstage. Alone.

Chapter Fourteen

The cast party was a joyless celebration for Paige. Well after dark, the shuttle returned her, Jamila, Jenny, and the Mias to the train, the older women gushing non-stop over Davyn's poem and the romance of that kiss.

Their first and last.

When they reached the train, Jenny helped them board via the rear open-air platform. "Congratulations again, Team Mias and Team Rhyme and Dine. You've secured a spot in the final draw for twenty-five thousand dollars."

"Is Davyn Kayne here?" the taller Mia asked. "I didn't get his autograph at the auditorium."

Jenny shook her head. "From what I've heard, he hasn't boarded, and I'm not expecting him. Not after that reception. Did you hear? Pop stars are clamoring for the rights to set his *Christmas for Me is You* poem to music." She beamed at Jamila. "I'm sure your excellent underscoring gave them the idea. So glad Davyn could coordinate that with you this morning."

Jamila grinned, then turned serious. "What about the Team S-s-stirs?" They'd left the party early.

"Sadly, they were caught cheating," Jenny reported.

"How?" the other women asked as a chorus.

"We discovered they'd built their sticky toffee pudding out of cardboard, filled it with hand weights to make it heavy, then covered it with cake and topping." Jenny shook her head. "Because of their deception, they've been disqualified and asked to leave the train."

On the platform, Paige saw the disgraced team members claiming their luggage. *How sad.* Then she saw them kiss and knew they'd be okay. Though no one could predict their futures, they had each other. Even the Mias were reunited. The two giggled together like teenagers as they boarded, whatever rift that had ruined their friendship, now mended.

Paige wished she could switch places with any of them.

"Cheer up, Paige," Jenny said. "You're a winner."

She sure didn't feel like one. Not even when Jenny surprised her with a paycheck for her work in the dining car the morning Bruce was left to serve single-handedly.

"Coming in?" Jenny asked.

Paige slipped the check into her pocket. "I'll stay out here for a bit. Get some air."

"Don't be too long, now. It's a chilly night." Jenny shivered, then disappeared inside the train.

But the cold suited Paige's mood.

Foolishly, secretly, she'd hoped Davyn would fall for her. But how could she compete with a legion of adoring fans? People smarter, more worldly, and better suited to match his intellect.

Paige could hardly blame him for choosing them over her. Today, she'd felt the thrill of the audience's approval, their applause warming her like the sun's beam on a tropical beach. She knew the cold of a crowd's disapproval too. Remembered it from the humiliations she'd suffered at school.

Davyn's public had rejected him once, and he still ran to them tonight. Just as he'd run off to help his parents after they'd discarded him.

Heck, she'd abandoned him too, hadn't she? Falsely accused him without knowing all the facts. But she'd admitted she was wrong and asked for his forgiveness. They'd even kissed. The memory of it made her stomach flutter and her pulse race.

How could he have shared such an intimate, intense moment with her and walked away? Didn't he realize she was right here, waiting for him, aching to hold him, kiss him, and give him a love that was real?

She brought a hand to her heart. Was that true? Did she really love him?

It hardly mattered now. He was gone, and she'd never get to say the words. Never get to prove it to him.

Maybe it was time to love herself first.

She remembered one of the songs she'd heard Jamila and her trio sing—*Feeling Good*. It was, indeed, *a new day*, and Paige needed to start fresh.

"I helped write a piece with a renowned poet. I *am* smart," she said aloud.

Maybe not in a scholastic way, but she was smart in a practical way. Still, she was going to face her demons and resolved to finish her high school diploma for her own sense of accomplishment. She'd use the check in her pocket toward her first course. Then she was going to take her savings, build on them, and buy her own restaurant.

Or maybe she'd train to become a speech therapist.

Despite her plans for a rosy future, she choked up when the whistle sounded, and the train began to roll out of the station. She'd never see Davyn again.

"Paige!"

Wow. She was so foolishly lovesick she'd even imagined hearing his voice. She turned to go inside, then heard her name called again.

She rushed to the railing and peered into the dark night. There, running along the platform, was the shadow of a person trying to catch the train.

"Davyn!"

She opened the safety gate and held out her hand to him. He reached for it...and missed.

Paige leaned out farther and stretched her arm as far as she could. Davyn reached for her hand a second time, caught it, and she helped pull him onto the platform and into her embrace. The pounding of his heart almost out-beat her own.

"I thought I'd never see you again."

"I won't lie," he gasped. "I was caught up in the moment after the performance. Caught up by the media attention and by the two signed contracts in my breast pocket." He patted them.

Regardless of where their relationship stood, she was proud of him. "Congratulations."

"I have you to thank for it. You're my muse."

She'd never been anyone's inspiration before. Did he mean it?

"But I accused you of something you didn't do. I was as bad as those reporters who wrote stories condemning you."

"That hurt. But you apologized, and I forgive you."

He kissed her temple, then her forehead, caressing her guilt away. His closeness healed the misunderstanding that had separated them. But one point still niggled at her.

"I'm not your only muse," she told him. "What about the audience? Wasn't their attention thrilling?"

"That was nice too. But, as the old saying goes, you can't take the audience home with you. That kind of faceless adoration isn't love. What I have with you is."

Had she heard him correctly? "Love?"

"I know we just met, but I've never felt this way about anyone before. You've helped me back on my feet, just like you said you would."

He stroked her cheek, then threaded his fingers through her hair. "I don't need anything...*anyone*...but you."

He kissed her. Slowly. Deeply. Thoroughly. It might have been cold on the platform, but Paige didn't feel it. Not when she was in Davyn's arms.

Like the Team Stirs, she knew they'd have challenges ahead but, together, they could overcome anything. They'd already proven it.

"I love you too. Merry Christmas, my darling," she told him.

All without stuttering.

Preview

Are you curious who the mysterious benefactor of this incredible train trip is? Who could possibly have enough money to fund a month-long trip for one hundred contestants and provide a twenty-five-thousand-dollar prize? Wonder why they'd be inspired to run such a contest.

Are you wondering how the train administrators knew that Dalton Wainwright shouldn't be without his dog, Grace? Are you curious about the reasons behind Tess Burton's breakup with the man she was seeing? Check out the next wonderful story, *On Board for Love*, written by Raine Hughes, as she follows The Rocky Mountain Christmas Train on its exciting journey toward Canada.

The Rocky Mountain Christmas Train Series

About Roxy Boroughs

Before launching her writing career, the multi-talented Roxy Boroughs was an accomplished stage and film actor who appeared in the TV series *Degrassi Junior High*; and top-rated movies such as *It Must Be Love*, starring Ted Danson and Mary Steenburgen.

Look for her romantic comedy *Crazy for Cowboy*, her suspense series *Psychic Heat*, featuring the award-winning novel *A Stranger's Touch*; and the popular *Frost Family Christmas* series, marrying sweet romance with cozy mystery.

Other heartwarming holiday titles include: *The Sprite Before Christmas*, *Capturing the Christmas Cowboy*, featured in *A Cowboy This Christmas: A Sweet Romance Anthology*, and *A Christmas*

Carole, featured in *Christmas Romance Digest 2021: Home for the Holidays,* edited by Tracy Cooper-Posey.

Roxy is married to her first love, so she not only writes romance, she lives it! If she's not typing away at her desk, she's reading, quilting, whipping up a fabulous new recipe, or hiking around the Rocky Mountain village she calls home, where mule deer and bighorn sheep roam the streets.

Where to Find Roxy

Website: https://www.roxyboroughs.com/
Email: https://roxy@roxyboroughs.com
Newsletter Sign-up: https://www.roxyboroughs.com/newsletter/
Facebook: https://www.facebook.com/RoxyBoroughsAuthor
https://www.facebook.com/roxy.boroughs
BookBub: https://www.bookbub.com/profile/roxy-boroughs
Instagram: https://www.instagram.com/roxyboroughsauthor/
X: https://x.com/RoxyBoroughs
Goodreads: https://www.goodreads.com/roxyborough

Books by Roxy Boroughs

The Frost Family Christmas Series
Home for Christmas
The Greatest Gift
Other Christmas Stories
The Sprite Before Christmas
Anthologies
Hugs, Kisses and Mistletoe Wishes
Christmas Romance Digest 2021: Home for the Holidays
A Cowboy This Christmas: A Sweet Romance Anthology
Stories of Chance Romance (a breast cancer fundraiser)
Psychic Heat Series
A Stranger's Touch
A Stranger's Kiss
A Stranger's Love
Psychic Heat Anthology
Stand Alone Novels
Wolfen Time
Crazy for Cowboy

www.ingramcontent.com/pod-product-compliance
Lightning Source LLC
Chambersburg PA
CBHW022041170626
46808CB00003B/1306